A MAGIC CIRCLE BOOK

DUCK IN THE PARK

DUCK IN THE DARK

by **EVE BEGLEY**
illustrated by **JON PROVEST**

THEODORE CLYMER
SENIOR AUTHOR, READING 360

GINN AND COMPANY
A XEROX EDUCATION COMPANY

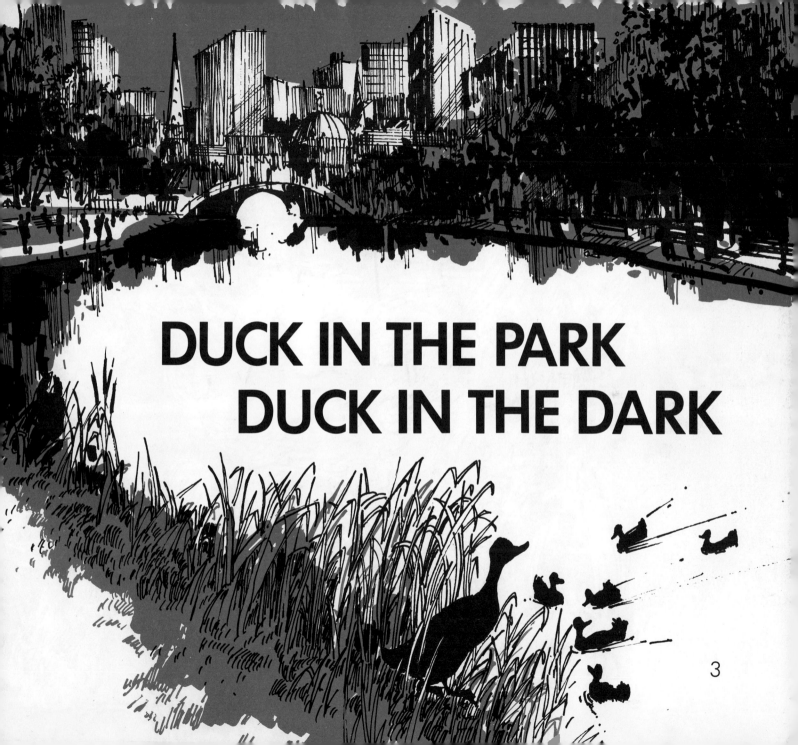

DUCK IN THE PARK
DUCK IN THE DARK

4

Duck in the park.

Duck in the dark.

6

Dog in the park.

Dog barks and barks.

7

8

Dog barks at the duck.

Duck hides in the park.

9

No help for the duck?

No help in the park?

Duck looks at the dog.

Dog runs in the dark.

12

13

No help for the dog?

No help in the park?

15

Quack! Quack! Quack!

CDEFGHIJK 765
PRINTED IN THE UNITED STATES OF AMERICA